S0-AEE-345

2022

PEDRO

THE
BEST PET?

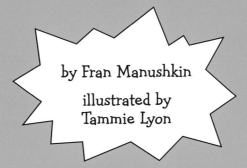

by Fran Manushkin

illustrated by
Tammie Lyon

PICTURE WINDOW BOOKS
a capstone imprint

Pedro is published by Picture Window Books,
an imprint of Capstone.
1710 Roe Crest Drive
North Mankato, Minnesota 56003
www.capstonepub.com

Text © 2021 Fran Manushkin
Illustrations © 2021 Picture Window Books

All rights reserved. No part of this publication may be reproduced in whole or in part, or stored in a retrieval system, or transmitted in any form or by any means, electronic, mechanical, photocopying, recording, or otherwise, without written permission of the publisher.

Cataloging-in-Publication Data is available on the Library of Congress website.
ISBN: 978-1-5158-7082-1 (library binding)
ISBN: 978-1-5158-7316-7 (paperback)
ISBN: 978-1-5158-7084-5 (eBook PDF)

Summary: Pedro and his dog, Peppy, are ready for the pet show. Peppy can sit and fetch on command. And he's freshly washed and ready to shine. But when they get to the pet show, Peppy gets upset and ends up in the mud. Is there any way for him to become the best pet?

Designer: Bobbie Nuytten
Design Elements: Shutterstock / Natasha Pankina

Printed and bound in the United States.
PA117

Table of Contents

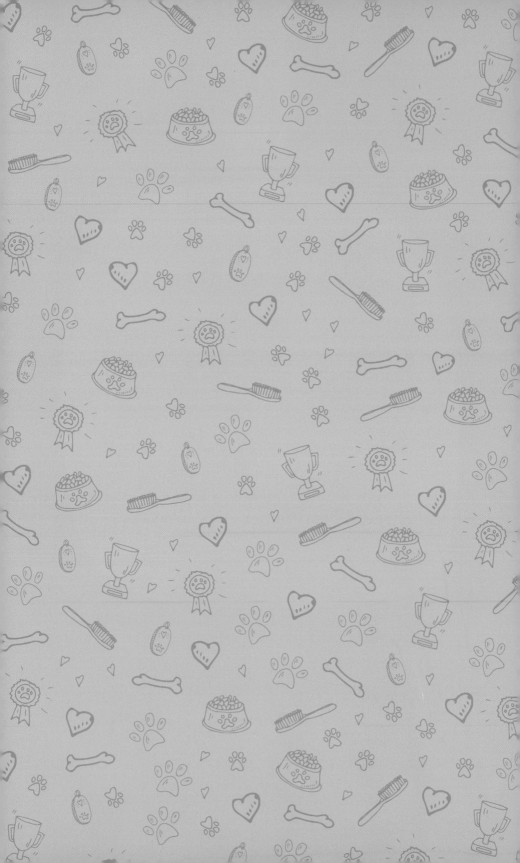

Chapter 1

Practice Time

Pedro told his dog, Peppy,

"Tomorrow is the pet show.

I want you to be the best pet!

Let's practice your tricks."

Pedro told Peppy, "Sit!"

Peppy sat.

Pedro said, "Stay."

Peppy stayed.

"Fetch!" said Pedro.

Peppy fetched.

"Good dog!" Pedro smiled.

He gave Peppy a treat.

Then Pedro gave Peppy a

bath.

Peppy did not like baths.

He liked mud a lot better!

Chapter 2
Show Day

The next day was the

pet show.

Pedro saw Katie and her

kitten, Peaches. Peppy liked

Peaches, and Peaches liked

Peppy.

Roddy told Pedro, "My parrot

Rocky will win. He is the best."

"Best! Best! BEST!" said Rocky.

Pedro waited for the judge

to come and see Peppy. Pedro

told Peppy, "Sit."

Peppy sat.

He sat on a bee.

TWO bees!

Peppy howled! Peppy jumped! Peppy ran!

He ran into a mud puddle.

SPLAT!

Peppy began to shake. He

shook mud all over Pedro.

"You two are a mess!" yelled

Roddy. "No ribbons for you."

Pedro felt sad.

Pedro tried to cheer up.

He watched Pablo's hamster

spinning on his wheel.

"Great spinning!" said the

judge.

Pablo won a ribbon.

Pedro saw JoJo and her
bunny, Betty.

Betty won a ribbon too. She
won for being soft and furry
and friendly.

Then Pedro saw Katie. She said, "Peaches is shaking. She has never been to a pet show. The noise and smells are scaring her."

The judges saw Roddy's parrot.

"He's the best," bragged Roddy.

Rocky screamed, "Best! Best!

BEST!"

That made

Peaches jump.

Peaches ran away!

Katie chased Peaches, but

Peaches was fast. She ran under

a fence and into the woods!

Chapter 3
Blue-Ribbon Winner

Peppy ran too! He ran after

Peaches.

Pedro yelled, "Peppy, FETCH!"

Peppy jumped over the fence.

Peaches was hiding. Peppy

sniffed and sniffed. He found

Peaches!

He picked her up and

jumped back over the fence.

SPLAT!

Peppy landed in the mud.

But he held on to Peaches.

She was safe!

Katie hugged Peaches and
Peppy. She didn't mind getting
muddy.

Pedro patted Peppy over and
over. "Good dog! Good dog!"

The judge told Pedro, "You told Peppy to fetch, and he did! Peppy is the best. He wins the blue ribbon!"

"Yay!" Everyone cheered.

When Pedro and
Peppy got home, they
needed a bath.

Guess who liked his
bath better?

About the Author

Fran Manushkin is the author of Katie Woo, the highly acclaimed fan-favorite early-reader series, as well as the popular Pedro series. Her other books include *Happy in Our Skin*, *Baby, Come Out!* and the best-selling board books *Big Girl Panties* and *Big Boy Underpants*. There is a real Katie Woo: Fran's great-niece, but she doesn't get into as much trouble as the Katie in the books. Fran lives in New York City, three blocks from Central Park, where she can often be found bird-watching and daydreaming. She writes at her dining room table, without the help of her naughty cats, Goldy and Chaim.

About the Illustrator

Tammie Lyon began her love for drawing at a young age while sitting at the kitchen table with her dad. She continued her love of art and eventually attended the Columbus College of Art and Design, where she earned a bachelor's degree in fine art. After a brief career as a professional ballet dancer, she decided to devote herself full time to illustration. Today she lives with her husband, Lee, in Cincinnati, Ohio. Her dogs, Gus and Dudley, keep her company as she works in her studio.

Glossary

brag (BRAG)—to talk in a boastful way about how good you are at something

fetch (FECH)—to go after and bring back something or somebody

howl (HOUL)—to cry out in pain or frustration

ribbon (RIB-uhn)—an award that is made out of a strip of colorful fabric

sniff (SNIF)—to smell for something

Let's Talk

1. How does Pedro feel after Peppy runs into the mud puddle? What clues tell you how he's feeling?

2. Do you agree that Peppy is the best pet? Why or why not?

3. Think of a pet you know, your own or someone else's. What would that pet win a ribbon for?

Let's Write

1. How did Pedro prepare Peppy for the pet show? List the steps.

2. List the pets in the story. Which would you like for a pet and why?

3. Make a blue ribbon for Peppy. On the ribbon, list reasons why Peppy is the winner.

JOKE AROUND

🌿 What is a dog's
favorite dessert?
Pupcakes!

🌿 Knock, knock.
Who's there?
Ken
Ken who?
Ken you walk the dog for me?

🌿 What do you call a pile of kittens?
A meowntain

🌿 Why are cats great
singers?
They are very mewsical.

WITH PEDRO!

🍁 What do you call a hamster with a top hat?
Abrahamster Lincoln

🍁 What was the bunny's favorite game?
Hopscotch

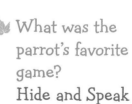

🍁 What was the parrot's favorite game?
Hide and Speak

HAVE MORE FUN WITH PEDRO!